DISCOVER DOGS WITH THE AMERICAN CANINE ASSOCIATION

I LIKE NORWICH TERRIERS!

Linda Bozzo

It is the mission of the American Canine Association (ACA) to provide registered dog owners with the educational support needed for raising, training, showing, and breeding the healthiest pets expected by responsible pet owners throughout the world. Through our activities and services, we encourage and support the dog world in order to promote best-known husbandry standards as well as to ensure that the voice and needs of our customers are quickly and properly addressed.

Our continued support, commitment, and direction are guided by our customers, including veterinary, legal, and legislative advisors. ACA aims to provide the most efficient, cooperative, and courteous service to our customers and strives to set the standard for education and problem solving for all who depend on our services.

For more information, please visit www.acacanines.com, email customerservice@acadogs.com, phone 1-800-651-8332, or write to the American Canine Association at PO Box 121107, Clermont, FL 34712.

Published in 2019 by Enslow Publishing, LLC.
101 W. 23rd Street, Suite 240, New York, NY 10011

Library of Congress Cataloging-in-Publication Data
Names: Bozzo, Linda, author.
Title: I like Norwich terriers! / Linda Bozzo.
Description: New York, NY : Enslow Publishing, 2019. | Series: Discover dogs with the American Canine Association | Includes bibliographical references and index. | Audience: Grades K to 3.
Identifiers: LCCN 2017045160| ISBN 9780766096714 (library bound) | ISBN 9780766096721 (pbk.) | ISBN 9780766096738 (6 pack)
Subjects: LCSH: Norwich terrier—Juvenile literature.
Classification: LCC SF429.N65 B69 2017 | DDC 636.755—dc23
LC record available at https://lccn.loc.gov/2017045160

Printed in the United States of America

To Our Readers: We have done our best to make sure all websites in this book were active and appropriate when we went to press. However, the author and the publisher have no control over and assume no liability for the material available on those websites or on any websites they may link to. Any comments or suggestions can be sent by email to customerservice@enslow.com.

Photo Credits: Cover, pp. 1, 13 (puppy), 18 violetblue/Shutterstock.com; p. 3 (left) Sbolotova/Shutterstock.com; p. 3 (right) Jne Valokuvaus/Shutterstock.com; p. 5 msupercolor/Shutterstock.com; p. 6 Zuzule/Shutterstock.com; p. 9 violetblue/Shutterstock.com; p. 10 Grossemy Vanessa/Alamy Stock Photo; p. 13 (collar) graphicphoto/iStock/Thinkstock, (bed) Luisa Leal Photography/Shutterstock.com, (brush) In-Finity/Shutterstock.com, (food and water bowls) exopixel/Shutterstock.com, (leash, toys) © iStockphoto.com/Liliboas; p. 14 Matthew Eisman/WireImage/Getty Images; p. 17 Steve Bruckmann/Shutterstock.com; p. 19 Capture Light/Shutterstock.com; p. 21 Natalia Fedosova/Shutterstock.com.

Enslow Publishing
101 W. 23rd Street
Suite 240
New York, NY 10011
USA
enslow.com

CONTENTS

IS A NORWICH TERRIER RIGHT FOR YOU?

Norwich terriers are little dogs full of energy. They don't like to sit around. If you are part of an **active** family, a Norwich terrier could be right for you.

The Norwich terrier and the Norfolk terrier look alike except for their ears. The Norwich terrier's ears stick up. The Norfolk terrier's ears hang down.

A DOG OR A PUPPY?

Norwich terriers are always ready to learn. But if you do not have time to train a puppy, you may want an older Norwich instead.

This breed is a natural hunter.

LOVING YOUR NORWICH TERRIER

Loving your Norwich terrier means spending lots of time with him. Play and cuddle with him. He's happy if he has a job to do.

Norwich terriers do well in dog sports, such as **flyball**.

EXERCISE

Norwich terriers need long walks on a leash. They enjoy games like fetch. They also like to explore the world around them.

A yard with fencing is best for your Norwich terrier.

FEEDING YOUR NORWICH TERRIER

Norwich terriers can be fed wet or dry dog food. Ask a **veterinarian** (vet), a doctor for animals, which food is best for your dog and how much to feed her.

Give your Norwich terrier fresh, clean water every day.

Remember to keep your dog's food and water dishes clean. Dirty dishes can make a dog sick.

Do not feed your dog people food. It can make her sick.

Your new dog will need:

a collar with a tag

a bed

a brush

food and water dishes

a leash

toys

The Norwich terrier should be groomed by a professional to take out dead hair at least twice a year.

GROOMING

Norwich terriers shed very little. This means their hair falls out but not a lot. Your Norwich terrier will need to be brushed often and bathed only when needed. Make sure you use shampoo made specially for dogs.

A Norwich terrier's nails will need to be clipped. A vet or groomer can show you how. Your dog's pointed ears should be cleaned, and his teeth should be brushed by an adult.

WHAT YOU SHOULD KNOW

Norwich terriers, like all terriers, like to dig holes outside. Keep your dog busy with play and exercise to stop her from doing this.

These dogs might chase small pets, but most get along with other dogs and cats.

Norwich terriers don't do well in the heat. Keep her cool on hot summer days.

You will need to take your new dog to the vet for a checkup. He will need shots, called **vaccinations**, and yearly checkups to keep him healthy. If you think your dog may be sick or hurt, call your vet.

A GOOD FRIEND

Your Norwich terrier can live as long as 14 years. During that time, she will enjoy being a friend to the whole family.

Norwich terriers are fun and loving toward children of all ages.

NOTE TO PARENTS

It is important to consider having your dog spayed or neutered when the dog is young. Spaying and neutering are operations that prevent unwanted puppies and can help improve the overall health of your dog.

It is also a good idea to microchip your dog, in case he or she gets lost. A vet will implant a microchip under the skin containing an identification number that can be scanned at a vet's office or animal shelter. The microchip registry is contacted, and the company uses the ID number to look up your information from a database.

Some towns require licenses for dogs, so be sure to check with your town clerk.

For more information, speak with a vet.

There are many dogs, young and old, waiting to be adopted from animal shelters and rescue groups.

Words to Know

active Always keeping busy.

fetch To go after a toy and bring it back.

flyball A dog sport where teams of dogs race, jump over hurdles, and then catch a ball launched into the air by a machine.

groomer A person who bathes and brushes dogs.

leash A chain or strap that attaches to the dog's collar.

shed When dog hair falls out so new hair can grow.

vaccinations Shots that dogs need to stay healthy.

veterinarian (vet) A doctor for animals.

Read About Dogs

Books

Casteel, Seth. *It's a Puppy's Life*. Washington, DC: National Geographic Children's Books, 2018.

McCardie, Amanda. *Our Very Own Dog: Taking Care of Your First Pet*. Somerville, MA: Candlewick Press, 2017.

Stoltman, Joan. *My First Dog*. New York, NY: Gareth Stevens Publishing, 2017.

Websites

American Canine Association Inc., Kids Corner

www.acakids.com

Visit the official website of the American Canine Association.

National Geographic for Kids, Pet Central

kids.nationalgeographic.com/explore/pet-central

Learn more about dogs and other pets at the official site of the National Geographic Society for Kids.

INDEX